What People Are Saying About

An Unholy Love

This beautifully written book **takes the reader on a spiritual odyssey** that transcends religious speculation in its apprehension of the imperishable power of love. The narrative breaks through the dark side of dying and death to realize an end both beautiful and spiritual. *An Unholy Love* is for anyone who fears the unknown, or is in doubt about their own salvation.

S. L. McCALLUM, *La Source*

An intimate, wide-ranging story that does not shirk to question many of religion's truths, without losing sight of man's ultimate destiny. The great value of this little book is that it **leads us to discover something about ourselves**, which, had we not turned its pages, might have lain undeveloped and unknown. This is a book that can be read many times over. I **could not put it down.**

J.L MOORE

This remarkable journal, written by a dying man in the last months of his life, is the record of a crisis of faith that forces him to reevaluate aspects of Christian dogma and doctrine. The experience of falling in love forces him to set aside earlier perspectives and assumptions, which result in a more profound understanding of the nature of love, life and death. **Beautifully written, and deeply moving**, *An Unholy Love* goes beyond conventional boundaries in its attempt to understand man in his wholeness.

O.M. KORTLANG

AN
UNHOLY
LOVE

VERNON L. ANLEY

RESOURCE *Publications* · Eugene, Oregon

Resource Publications
A division of Wipf and Stock Publishers
199 W 8th Ave, Suite 3
Eugene, OR 97401

Acknowledgments

I would like to thank Raymond Zala, who has made time, in the course of the very busy life he leads, to read the typescript with meticulous care, and for the many suggestions that have improved the flow of material and ensured factual accuracy.

Jesus cried out and said,
"Whoever believes in me
Does not believe in me,
but in him who sent me."
JOHN: 12:44

ഇൻ

After this life
God himself is our place.
SAINT AUGUSTINE

LONDON

September 20

A bbot Brennan asked me to keep a diary, recording not every event, but what seemed important, significant, new. He also asked me to reflect on my years at St. Benedict Monastery. Much is too obvious to be mentioned, too recurrent to be thought worth recording. But I now see that earlier events that I thought insignificant were important, and judgments made at the time need to be qualified and corrected. If this diary is not to be a narrative of bald facts, I must not only set down what I feel and imagine, but also make sense of what I had hitherto experienced but not properly understood.

Time is not a matter of great importance at St. Benedict. As we are called to a routine of prayer and meditation, the objects of experience change slowly and in expected ways. But beyond the walls of the monastery, time is a whirligig; the objects of experience change rapidly and in novel, unexpected ways. I have no idea where the next few months will take me, or what to expect. It is quite unnerving....

$$\mathcal{SOCR}$$

Turning to the past, I recognize that the death of my grandfather when I was a boy was a turning point in my life. I saw his body, but where was he? Something essential was missing. His death was a sudden transition from vitality and vigor to silence. He could no longer be reached by words, and this was not something transitory, but final. His time on earth was over. Where to now? The body being buried was his, but where was the person I knew him to be? That death is something natural and taken for granted does not cancel out its existential incomprehensibility. My grandfather's death made Christ's resurrection decidedly possible.

Another hugely important event was meeting Father Lucian. He was a born teacher as well as a priest. At a very early age he was sent to the abbey of Monte Cassino for elementary schooling, and then to the University of Naples, where he entered the Jesuit order. After a period of teaching in Genoa and Rome, he was sent to Australia. He expected to teach at a seminary but found himself posted to a suburban church in Melbourne. It was a fortunate decision for our parish. He engaged the church in our daily lives and was devoted to serving the needs of our community.

During the school holidays I helped Father Lucian with his pastoral duties. In return he taught me about the church and its liturgies, its doctrines and religious orders, and most importantly, that beside the factual knowledge reached through experience, there is another kind of knowledge born of love: the kind Pascal spoke of when he said that the heart has reasons which reason does not know.

Until I met Father Lucian, the little religious instruction I had received came from my mother. Like many of my generation I was brought up far from the Sunday-school atmosphere of conventional religiosity. From my earliest years I was led to feel that religion is a personal matter. I accepted the creed set before me, but outside the home I would never have invoked religious grounds for my actions.

My parents were as surprised as I was when Father Lucian told them I had a religious vocation. He said that my tendency for solitude and meditation was a gift of the Spirit, although I never saw it in this light. On the other hand, I was always aware that there was something greater than the physical world, something which I was happy to call God, and which had a distinct dimension of its own.

I have never been able to explain my feelings for God in

rational terms. The heart hears the great things that happen to us, the experiences we do nothing to arrange but live by, and the head often finds it difficult to follow up with a rational explanation. God calls those he chooses to call, however unlikely it may appear. *"God will have mercy on whom He will have mercy; so then it is not of him that willeth, not of him that runneth, but of God that showeth mercy."* I neither "willeth" nor did I "run" but was "taken up" by his mercy.

By the time I left school I knew I wanted to give my life to this unknown God who had entered my life.

I entered the Seminary of St. Columbanus, one of the teaching institutions of the College of Divinity in Melbourne, a few weeks after my eighteenth birthday. St. Columbanus was one of the great missionaries of the Celtic church. His monastery in the small town of Bobbio in northern Italy was famous for its library. When the monastery declined in the fifteenth century the library was dispersed, most of its 700 manuscripts going to the Vatican. The Holy See gave the Seminary some of Columba's poems and a penitential, which are kept under glass in a sanctuary near the chapel. One of his poems begins with the line, "When my spirit grows faint within me, it is you who knows the way." It has stayed in my mind, and I have had cause to remember it often.

Our studies included an introduction to the Old and New Testament, Social Ethics, the History of Christianity, and courses related to the ministry and pastoral counselling. Only in my last year, when we studied St. Paul's teaching in detail did the gospel narrative come to life. No one taught St. Paul about Jesus. *"For I would have you know, brethren, that the gospel preached by me is not according to man, for I did not receive it from man but through a revelation of Jesus Christ."* Free to realize a vision, intensified by the concentrated energy of his restless spirit, he turned Jesus into a cosmic figure.

Christ's transition from the veiled glory of the cross to the open glory of the resurrection is like the transition from darkness to light. Where Christ has gone we also go. What he has pioneered we also experience. It is a powerful and exciting set of images, and I fell under their spell.

Towards the end of my final year I knew that I wanted to join a monastic order. Until then I had not thought of entering a monastery, let alone taking a vow of poverty, chastity, and obedience. The church needed people to work in hospitals, to teach the catechism, to preach and dispense the sacraments, and I was happy to follow any of these vocations. The words of the old desert fathers *"fuge, tace, et quiesce"* (live in solitude, silence, and inner peace) were far from my mind. But Jesus required complete emancipation from all ties of this world. There was only one community whose virtues demanded the necessary solitude and silence: the Order of the Cistercians of the Strict Observance. As the Cistercian Abbey in the Yarra

Valley was still under construction, I chose to enter St. Benedict in the English Cotswolds.

ℰꙹℭꙶ

Saying good-bye to those you love is never easy; it is even harder when you know that you might not see them again. Nothing had really prepared me for this moment. When I said good-bye to my family for the last time it struck me that this parting was possibly final. For nearly everyone there is unfinished business when they leave home. In my case I knew there was little chance of return or redress.

I received several letters from Abbot Reumann, who was then in his sixties, telling me about St. Benedict: its location in the English countryside, and its dedication to the Statutes of the Cistercian Order. Life in the monastery, he said, had only one purpose, to realize a more and more intimate union with God or, as the Statute put it, "To seek God with more passion and fervour in one's heart and soul, to find him as soon as possible and possess him more than perfectly."

Life was entirety consecrated to God's contemplation through prayer, spiritual reading, and meditation. It would be my vocation, he said, to live in silence and in the solitude of the cell. "To pray fruitfully one must head for solitude and stillness, and to recollect oneself from the scramble of everyday life." As for my faith, he said it must have the certitude of an invisible truth, "analogous on the human level, to the silent beating of one's heart." I was in no doubt about my faith and willingly accepted the devotional exercises demanded of me.

ℬℭ

I arrived in England in February after six weeks aboard the *Oriana*. After the sunlight of an Australian summer the gray-green landscape, obscured in part by fog and cloud, was colorless and cold. St. Benedict isolated and secluded, its stone walls draped in mist, looked austere but compelling. As I approached the monastery, it dawned upon me that this was my last hour in the world as I knew it. But I had no misgivings. I felt I had reached my spiritual home.

The train from Paddington had taken longer than expected because of the snow. By the time Brother Anthony, the novice master, had introduced me to the Abbot and shown me to my cell, the monks had finished their evening meal and were saying Compline. The sound of their voices echoed through the monastery. We tend to think of the institutional as impersonal, but there was nothing impersonal about those voices.

The hours of common worship soon became the high

point of my day. Standing on either side of the simple tabernacle we sang the psalms with all the ardor our hearts could muster. The acoustics of our little chapel are extraordinary. A single voice was an instrument of song. Two or three voices were a choir, and a choir became an orchestra. When we sang the *"Te Deum,"* it was as rousing as the "Hallelujah Chorus."

෫෧෬

The following morning Father Anthony introduced me to the other monks. In less than a hundred years the population of St. Benedict had fallen from more than sixty monks to just eleven. Perhaps we have become something of an anachronism. Thomas Aquinas, himself a Dominican friar, said that we should share the fruits of contemplation with others. It is better, he said, for the "candle to give light than just to burn." But we do shed light in our own way, and if it is sometimes hidden, so are the sun's rays, but the light still shines.

It took me several days to get to know the labyrinth of passageways linking our cells to the cloister, library, and chapel. Before the modernizing reforms of the second Vatican Council we slept in common dormitories. Now we each have our own small room, which is just large enough for a bed, a desk, and a chair. Each room has a single window above the line of sight to avoid the temptation to distraction. The only concession to excess is a candle that burns day and night in a niche in the wall of each cell. Benedictines reject ornamentation and figurative art. Even our crosses are bare in obedience to St. Benedict's dictum that "pictorial characters represent a distraction more than an incentive to inspiration."

Within the walls of the monastery, behind the chapel, in an area not much larger than a small garden, is the graveyard. There are no headstones: the Abbot has to update the plan of the cemetery after each burial. It is a small plot. We lie in our brothers' sod.

During my first few weeks I learned the code of duty that regulates our lives. The Rule of St. Benedict extends to seventy-three chapters. For the novice, the most important is the call for a full year's probation, followed by a solemn vow of obedience to the Rule as mediated by the Abbot and a vow of lifelong residence. "Against the power and delight of the temporal one must set the joy of the eternal," said St. Benedict, "and against the passion of the sensual the ecstasy of the spiritual."

It is a steep climb. Only gradually is the undeniable reality of the one matched by the compelling power of the other.

LONDON

September 21

My flight has been delayed another day. The strike in Paris continues.

In the monastery one maintains his connection with the past as best he can, while ceaselessly pulling away from it. To remain in touch with the past requires a love of memory and imaginative effort, neither of which are facilitated by long periods of prayer and meditation. After a while time becomes an abstraction, absorbed in a sort of indefinite present that encompasses both past and future. Clock time has very different frames of reference. It is more immediate, static, and isolated. It will take getting used to.

Before Brother Anthony put a finger to my lips, engaging my lifelong vow to speak only in prayer, he asked how I might contribute to our upkeep. Labor is not a pecuniary necessity.

The monastery supports itself by leasing large tracts of land accumulated over many centuries, thanks to the diligence of our forebears. But the Bible says that man should *"eat the labour of thine hands,"* so we add toil to our daily contemplation. I told Father Anthony I had taken carpentry lessons at school. Suffice it to say, without test or trial, I became the keeper of the hammer and saw.

Life in St. Benedict is not as solitary as one might imagine. The sense of community is encouraged by the arrangement of the cells, which although separated from one another are linked by a single cloister. Our day begins at midnight when we gather in silence to sing the Liturgy of Hours. In the pre-dawn shadows following the Liturgy we return to our cells to rest before rising for the recitation of the First Hour. After breakfast we go to our appointed tasks till Terce and the midday chanting of the canonical hours of Sext and None. The afternoon is taken up with work, prayer, and meditation. Dinner is followed by Vespers and individual prayer. Our day ends with the recitation of the Angelus, devotion in memory of the Incarnation recited as versicle.

Not every order is so dedicated to prayer, meditation, and study. We obey the Rule in the service of God, believing that compliance ensures we put our own interests aside. This is not to say that we lived like hermits, subjecting ourselves to permanent withdrawal. We eat together in the refectory, say mass together in the chapel, and walk with each other once a week outside the walls of the cloister. Alone, perhaps, but never lonely.

Learning that community is where community happens was one of my earliest lessons. A community is not just an aggregate of individuals, but an achievement of common meaning whereby one recognizes a common direction in one's living. Such community invites expression. We called it love, but *"mutual indwelling"* is the better term. It is not possessive, exclusive, or particular, but neither is it impersonal or an act of obedience. It comes from living the first and the greatest of God's commandments. The second, love your neighbor, follows naturally.

I was a novice for two years, after which I took my vows, promising a lifetime commitment to monastic life. This promise was celebrated by a special mass led by the Abbot. As I listened to him speak the words of Isaiah, *"Thus says the Lord: By waiting and calm, you shall be saved. In quiet and trust lies your strength,"* I knew I had found my vocation. I felt a happiness quite unlike anything I had experienced before: independent of affections and emotions, it was personal and compelling, almost as if it belonged to another order of experience.

After mass Father Anthony gave me the clothes I would wear for the next twenty years: mantle, cowl, leather belt, scapular and sandals. Putting on our common vesture marked the end of my previous life in civil society. Henceforth I was bound to a community that modeled its behavior on the self-giving of Christ.

Although sex had played little part in my life before I entered the monastery, my desires were not entirely forsaken. During the day I was able to put aside suggestive images, but night relaxed my preconscious censorship. After several months the claims ignored during the day made themselves felt in dream.

I dreamt of a young woman with dark brown eyes and snow-white skin. She came to me soon after sleep, inviting me into her arms. We embraced, and with murmured words, gave ourselves to each other. Her face was familiar, but I could not place her.

During the day she broke into my prayers, my meditations, my devotions. At night I called her into my arms. Enigmatic and beautiful, she shared my life...until I saw her.

In a niche in the refectory was a faded painting of the Blessed Virgin with St. Cosma standing beside her. It is the only painting in the monastery. Because it is above the line of sight and in shadow it is easily missed. When I saw the painting again, I was struck dumb. The Blessed Virgin was the girl in my dreams. The shock of embracing the Virgin put an end to my erotic dreams and all thought of sex generally.

PARIS

September 23

Arrived in Paris yesterday evening.

My hotel is in the Rue Volney, near the Jardin des Tuileries. It is not yet daybreak. The glow from a neon light across the street breaks into my room and blooms into a soft fluorescence. Even at this hour I can hear the noise of the traffic and rumble of underground trains. Paris, like all big cities, never sleeps. In St. Benedict the hours before dawn are a call to prayer and meditation. Now I find them tediously long. I find myself waiting for morning.

My tumor is quite visible now. It is below the waistline, adding slightly to my girth, but unnoticeable when I am dressed. Some sixth sense told me at the time that it was inoperable, and so it turned out to be. When one hears the verdict of death, a feeling of disbelief protects you from admitting the worst. It is only later, when you realize that death will do away with everything you love, that one feels threatened by anxiety: the confrontation with nothingness and the awesome unknowability of death.

Montaigne believed that death is easiest for those who during their lives have given it the most thought since they are most prepared for it. We, disciples of St. Benedict, should be better prepared than most, since we think of death more or less constantly (the crucified Christ is always before our eyes). We believe that the resurrection is God's corrective to the negative of death. We do not accept its finality. I still believe this, but more from spiritual instinct (surely not given in vain), than resurrection stories. But this does not lessen the anxiety about dying.

Such are the disturbing elements of guilt that I thought I had brought this sickness upon myself. For simultaneous with my illness, I lost faith in Jesus. It was too improbable that a man, one of us, had made his way to the supreme heights, beyond the angelic world, to the holy of holies, to become one with God. None are likely to believe too little as those who have begun by believing too much.

I had believed all that the Church would have me believe about Jesus: his incarnation, his resurrection, his miracles, and his messianic titles. St. Augustine flatly stated that there were many other ways in which God could redeem man apart from the suffering and death of Christ. Jesus lost his eschatological significance when I came to the same conclusion. His resurrection was not history remembered, but prophecy "historicized."

There is a notable anonymity to the gift of faith. Like the Johannine *pneuma*, it blows where it wills; you hear the sound of it, but you do not know where it comes from or where it is going. There is no fixed rule of antecedence and consequence, no necessity of simultaneity, no prescribed magnitude of change. Christ's fall from grace, in my case, was as sudden as it was unexpected. Job was made to suffer the tortures of the dammed merely to test his constancy. Did I deserve any better?

PARIS

September 25

I would be hard put to give an exact idea of my state of mind at the moment. The multitude of new things and new people that I have seen in the last few days, added to the uprooting of my own world, has left me rather dazed. I haven't yet managed to master or digest the mass of impressions that I have briefly and superficially come up against. When I successfully navigate back to my hotel, after taking a short walk, I feel as proud as if I had circumnavigated the globe.

Paris seems to be moving at an unnatural pace. Perhaps because of the giddy rush, people hardly notice one another: sometimes it is little more than a glance exchanged between strangers as they pass each other. Although I am familiar with the signs of address, I am quite happy that nothing is required of me and I can remain the background.

The cloister has made me wary about mixing with others, and of speaking unless necessary. Words still rightly belong to prayer. And yet I do not think my years in St. Benedict have made it difficult for me to engage with people. It is a mistake to think that solitude leads away from humanity. Even Jesus is described as reaching humankind through the wilderness.

Paris

September 26

I would like to explore Paris on foot.

Although I don't trust myself to walk for any length of time, I am determined to see as much as I can. Before Abbot Reumann died, he told me that we should be grateful for circumstances that force one to do something we would not have done otherwise. With these words in mind, I have made a list of places to visit and things to do.

Moments before Abbot Reumann died we were called to his bedside. Father Anthony indicated the time for the last sacrament by holding up his left hand with the palm up and drew a cross on it with the tip of his right thumb. At the moment of death he placed the tip of his right thumb under the Abbot's chin and raised it slightly. The Abbot died with a look of heaven on his face, as if eternity was just a heartbeat away.

After washing his body we dressed him in habit, scapular, and cowl, and carried him into the chapel, where we laid his body on a bier facing the altar. Following a requiem mass we carried his body from the chapel and lowered it into the grave with two bands of white linen. Father Anthony asked God to have mercy on his soul, *"Domine miserere super peccatrice..."* And that was the end.

Death brings sadness and loss but does not cancel the memory of times spent together, or that feeling of "presence" that sustains our connection with those who have died. Even so I miss the Abbot greatly. Unafraid of the world and at peace with God, he called us to follow the path of love. "Love," he told me, "represents the heart of the Divine. Life will be meaningless for you if you do not reach into it with all the love that you can; in this way you will discover its meaning for yourself. Meet the world with the fullness of your being, and you shall meet God. If you wish to believe, love."

At the time I thought his words were an encouragement to greater devotion. I gave myself wholly to prayer and meditation, but the divine Son was nowhere to be found, or I could not find him. It became impossible for me to say Christ's name with any sincerity. Words, previously spoken with conviction, became insubstantial and sterile, empty of the truth that gave them meaning. Gradually this malaise extended its range, like spreading rust so that prayer and worship became meaningless and penance impossible. Like Job, I half expected God to come riding along on the tempest of his almightiness and thunder reproaches, *"Who is this that darkens counsel by words without insight?"*

St. Ignatius, in the Spiritual Exercises, urges us, when contemplating Christ, to do one's own thinking. In my case, the outcome was entirely unexpected. I wanted to rest content with faith, but faith broke faith with me. It was impossible to conceive Jesus as a God, or even God's Son, *"by whom are all things, and we by him."*

How could that which creates and sustains the universe be reduced to the infinitesimal human scale? Or a man be so elevated that he becomes capable of grounding the explanation of everything in the universe? I became painfully, almost despairingly conscious of the fact that I had crossed the boundary from belief to unbelief. Although I still find it difficult to accept, I have a feeling that ultimately much more will be realized than lost.

PARIS

September 27

It started to rain early this morning. It has continued intermittently all day.

The hotel has a small library of English books. I am reading a translation of André Gide's *Journals*. The first entry includes a quote from Balzac's *Père Goriot*. It describes the moment Rastignac looks down on Paris from the heights of Père Lachaise, and cries, "And now...you and I come to grips!" I feel something of the same excitement as I look over the rooftops towards Sacre Coeur. Although I cannot walk far, I have every intention of seeing as much as I can. Tomorrow, weather permitting, I will visit Notre Dame.

Notre Dame has three of Christ's relics: the Crown of Thorns, which was put on Jesus' head when he proclaimed himself King of the Jews, a piece of the original cross, and one of the nails that attached him to it. Whether they are genuine or not is immaterial. For believers, they are an evocation of Christ, who, taking his departure from this world, entered the presence of God. We owe their significance to St. Paul. If Paul had not had his recognition experience, it is unlikely that Jesus would be remembered, or, if remembered at all, merely as the founder of an obscure sect whose execution was carried out without fanfare.

Paul was not mad, as Festus thought, when he heard about Paul's vision of the risen dead. But given Paul's neurotic temperament and the stress of persecuting the Christians, his hallucinatory experience would have affected his rationality. What actually happened on the road to Damascus must remain a mystery, unless we accept Paul's own account, *"I was laid hold of by Jesus Christ."*

In any event, the reality and the mental image fused to create an experience that convinced him Jesus was alive, *"raised from the dead and died no more."* Before his conversion Paul thought it absurd to maintain that God had intervened to raise from the dead a false teacher whose blasphemous claim to be the Messiah was a deliberate subversion of the Law. But after his Damascus experience, he accepted Jesus' resurrection, which he had contemptuously dismissed, as a fact. Jesus, crucified under Pontius Pilate, was the Son of God! It was a remarkable *volte face.* Christians now had an advocate in heaven who promised access to God and eternal life.

St. Paul is the supreme mystagogue. His conviction that Jesus' death lead to a corporeal resurrection in God assumes a radical mysticism of union that rejects human nature. It is beyond comprehension, ecstatic, and awe-inspiring.

But whatever we make of it, the fact remains that God, who calls us up out of nothing, who is Being and Life itself, needs no avatar to unite us with himself. *"For there is no other save me; I am Alpha and Omega, the beginning and the end, the first and the last."*

PARIS

September 28

Early this morning the air was full of pale blue, which seemed to moisten the horizon like milk. But it did not last. As soon as I left the hotel, it started to rain. Although it has cleared somewhat, dark clouds still loiter over the city. Another day indoors.

I am still thinking about the events of the last few months.

It is not just personal doubt that undermines beliefs and values. It can be that they lose their original power, or no longer answer fundamental questions about life and death. This can happen because the conditions of the present period are very different from those in which the spiritual contents were created. Our world is not one of apocalyptic expectation, where the miraculous is not only credible, but expected. In the spiritual climate in which Jesus lived, people were awaiting a Messiah who would magically transform the whole human situation.

Mark's summary of Christ's preaching, *"And saying, 'The time is fulfilled, and the kingdom of God is at hand,'"* assumes that the time had come. The wicked would be punished, and the righteous would "arise," transported into a heavenly mode of being. But the Messiah who came did nothing startling to transform the world. Like the prophets before him who believed that God's rule was imminent, Jesus was mistaken in thinking that the *"end time"* was near.

Believing there was still some event that must take place first, namely, that he, the messiah-to-be, must sacrifice himself (as prophesized by Isaiah) as atonement for those who would follow him, Jesus journeyed to Jerusalem to put himself in the hands of his enemies. The Sanhedrin had Jesus arrested for blasphemy (a capital crime under Jewish law), claiming to be the Messiah and Son of God. Because the death penalty was not an option for the Sanhedrin under Roman law, he was brought before Pilate for sentencing.

Pilate acceded to the urgings of the Jewish leaders to crucify Jesus because he feared that any movement with a promise of apocalyptic intervention posed a threat to Roman rule. Pilate asked Jesus if he was *"King of the Jews."* His answer, *"You have said it,"* permits Jesus to stand silent before his accusers as prescribed by prophecy and ensures him a death sentence by crucifixion for the crime of sedition.

Although both the day and the hour that Jesus died are unknown, it is almost certain that he was not placed in a tomb when he expired. The Romans did not bury executed prisoners but dumped them together in mass graves. There was no splendor and glory hovering over Jesus' burial, no gifts of myrrh and aloes. After the most wretched and ignominious of deaths, he had the most miserable and wretched of burials.

For the Romans the "Jesus case" was finally closed, and there it might have ended...but for Paul. On the evidence of his revelatory experience he believed that Jesus had risen from the dead and was *"set at the right hand of God."* Paul bestowed on Jesus the titles and authority that previously had been God's alone: everything in the universe must acknowledge the sovereignty, the lordship of the exalted Jesus. To make the improbable possible he created a myth that transformed Jesus' death into a salvation event. As Christ was dead so he became alive; for those who appropriate his death to themselves their own death is also overcome.

While Paul's words show how historically conditioned situations can influence even a basic dogma like the resurrection, his vision of the resurrected Christ is a remarkable *tour de force*. His apocalyptic imagery is a captivating picture of heavenly power that rescues man from the powers of darkness "*to the kingdom of his beloved Son,*" where he will see God's countenance and rule for all eternity. But for all Paul's spiritual ingenuity and persuasion, his apocalyptic visions and pictorial language, there is only one God, and he needs no intermediary to do his bidding. "*I alone am God, the Creator of all, and apart from me there is no other.*"

PARIS

September 29

Sometimes we must abandon a particular belief in order to realize another whose value is higher still. It is the demand God made on Abraham when he called him to abandon the *"other gods"* his father served, and it is the demand Jesus delivered to his disciples: *"He that believeth on me, believeth not on me, but on him that sent me."* It was a summons largely ignored. In three instances John actually calls Jesus *"God."* Like the sun when the moon comes between it and the earth, God is eclipsed by his Son and disappears into the background.

Is it because of God's "invisibleness" that we find it necessary to make one of our own the center of religious life? With Jesus, one of us has made his way to the supreme heights, beyond the angelic world, to the holy of holies, where

God dwells. *"He has entered heaven itself, now to appear in the presence of God on our behalf."*

Only now can man's cause be pleaded at the highest level by man himself. Only then is there an end to utopian futures, and the promise of eternal salvation. But the risk of such intercession is that the face of Christ is superimposed over the face of God.

PARIS

September 29

Iplanned to visit Notre Dame this morning but got no further than the end of the street when the clouds broke. I entered a café to escape the rain. It was crowded and noisy. I ordered a coffee and felt quite at ease. This event, remarkable only for its banality, struck me as one of considerable daring. I am trusting myself to live in the world again.

PARIS

September 30

The great disadvantage of having so much time to myself is that I am constantly drawn back to the past.

When the Abbé Brennan became Abbot after the death of Abbé Reumann, I was obliged to tell him not only about my illness, but also my rejection of Jesus as a divine being. The disclosures came as something of a shock.

There is little one can say about death because it remains silent in itself. When I try and imagine my own death, the whole structure of understanding collapses, and there is no possibility of words breaching the gap. It is the vanishing point of all experience. After telling him that I had but a few months to live, we sat in silence for a while, a silence that was both a testimony of friendship and an expression of helplessness.

When he turned to the question of my faith, he told me

that the life and death of Jesus meant not only what he (Jesus) said it meant, but also what it was found to mean, and that I should reflect on this. He quoted St. Paul's message to the Corinthians, *"But to us there is but one God, the Father, of whom are all things, and we in him; and one Lord Jesus Christ, by whom are all things, and we by him,"* and said that both statements belong together and could not be played off one against the other. This is strong doctrine, but it does not free one from making his own judgments (for example, with reference to Paul's statement, how their relation to one another is to be understood).

Almost as an afterthought, the Abbot said that I might benefit from a short sabbatical. "It would do you no harm," he said, "to participate in the world again: to be tempted by other possibilities, to see things from another perspective, and remember the past."

This was a very unorthodox proposal, but I agreed.

Paris

October 1

It is surprising how often, during the most critical moments of life, everything hangs on chance.

Yesterday as I crossed the little garden in front of Notre-Dame I felt a sudden pain and stumbled to my knees. A young woman who was passing turned to help me. The spasm lasted only a minute, but without her help, I would have had difficulty getting to my feet. I thanked her, and thinking to send her a card or some flowers, asked her name and how I might reach her.

❧☙

This morning I bought Kim, for that is her name, a dozen roses, and on impulse took them to her myself. I don't know what possessed me to be so bold. I still feel unprepared to engage with people on a personal level. The different ways of addressing people, the phrases of everyday conversation, do not come easily.

Kim met me at the door. She is very slim, her step light, her movements graceful. Her hands are small, soft, delicate, and disappeared into mine when we shook hands. I felt a quickening pleasure when our fingers touched. This emotion is a new sensation for me. I'm not sure what to make of it.

Her apartment is like a jewel case. There is a lot of red velvet and gilt. The light was so softened and dimmed that it gave the illusion of night. On a black lacquer table in the sitting room was a large bronze Buddha sitting on a lotus blossom. It took center stage, the main actor among a cast of smaller Buddhas and bodhisattvas scattered about the room. The air smelt faintly of jasmine. The atmosphere was relaxing and seductive.

For two people who find silence more congenial than speech, we were very loquacious. I told Kim about my childhood in Australia, and the urgent expectation of finding God, which brought me to St. Benedict. I also told her I had cancer, about my apostasy, and that I had not long to live.

From what she told me about herself she has had little harmony or love in her life. Her mother was a Vietnamese refugee who became pregnant during her internment in

Toulouse. She left the camp when Kim was six months old and married a Malay Chinese who had a tailor's shop in the slums of the nineteenth arrondissement. Her mother left home when Kim was three. She was brought up by her stepfather, who returned to Malaysia when she was sixteen. Her only inheritance was her stepfather's religion, Hinayanian Buddhism.

Hinayanian Buddhists suppress all desires, even those we think of as altruistic, such as love and pity. This cold spirituality derives from a belief in an *"Absolute"* that is detached from the affairs of man. Kim's stepfather practiced what he preached. He abandoned her when he returned to Malaysia, leaving Kim penniless and without a home. She lived in hostels, moving repeatedly from one to the other, disqualified by this or that regulation, begging to be made an exception. Sometimes she was allowed to clean or cook without wages in return for a bed. Every time she changed hostels she lost the few friends she had made.

Without money she was under constant threat of being sent to prison. When she was caught traveling without a ticket on the metro she was put before the children's court and spent forty-eight hours in a police cell. Not long after this her purse was snatched, losing everything she had left in the world. Her social worker refused her any more food coupons and the hostel asked her to leave. She was just seventeen. Convinced that there was no point in living, she decided to throw herself off the Pont Neuf. She was stopped on the bridge by a man who offered her money for sex. She had nothing to lose.

When I returned to my hotel I could not sleep. I still cannot sleep. I cannot stop thinking about her. When I told her about life in the monastery, she said that there must have been times when I felt very alone. But after listening to Kim, I realized that it is a solitary act, in many cases, just to be human.

PARIS

October 9

I see Kim every day.

Despite the difference in our ages (she is just twenty-four, almost half my age), we get on very well together. To outsiders it may seem that we have nothing in common, but this is not so. Neither of us has lived a normal life. Neither of us knows the world in an undistorted form, or the more intimate aspects of human love. In the normal course of events I would not have expected to meet anyone whose life, like my own, has been marginalized in some way.

Today after lunch we walked along the Quai des Tuileries. The afternoon light unrolled in streams, giving the air a magical quality. When we reached the Terrasse, I was out of breath and had to rest. We sat down, and Kim took my hand. This gesture, so ordinary in itself, brought to consciousness what we felt for one another. It surprised us both. At that moment I knew that if we were not yet in love with each other, the time would not be long in coming.

Kim hoped for happiness, but so far happiness has visited her only in rare moments. Buddhist fatalism has ironed out the pain of her worst experiences, but she has little trust in the future. A world made up of casual relationships and transitory encounters does little to inspire hope or confidence. The discovery of common suffering brings people together. It brought us together. It is too early to say where it will lead, but I feel there is much that we can give one another.

PARIS

October 13

Everything seems so new to me today that I feel as if I am the first to see it.

Something has changed in me. I feel more alive, happier, and stronger. My feet scarcely touch the ground. I have the illusion that everything is wonderful, and that life, for some reason, is twice as well worth living. These feelings started with unabated keenness from the moment I met Kim.

I never imagined, let alone hoped, or expected, to find love. Perhaps when such things happen we should not look for answers, but count our blessings and be thankful.

PARIS

October 17

K im has suggested that I live with her.
I told her that cancer has no happy ending, that relief is fleeting and does nothing to lessen the distress it might temporarily displace. But she said this makes no difference. And so it was agreed. I left the hotel this morning. We are now living together. Just to say these words sounds extraordinary. The circumstances were so unforeseen, the possibility so unexpected, that the reality of living with her has yet to sink in.

I do not think that I am confusing love with sex. Sex is not something that springs to mind when you have given up all thought of it, and your libido is ill equipped to express it. Love is, above all, the gift of oneself, and if this gift is complete, sex is not necessary for its physical expression.

Aquinas said that fate was the action of God's providence, and perhaps it is. We both feel that the circumstance of our meeting was the result of a coming together of events that neither of us could have expected. I feel my heart swinging like a censor before me, rising into a world of happiness and love.

PARIS

October 20

These have been gloriously happy days. The only shadow is the knowledge that they cannot last. I would hold everything I see in the palm of my hand. We are not always aware of our having to die, but in that light our whole life is experienced differently. How much we miss when we take life for granted.

Although God alone knows how long I have to live, I am reminded daily that I am fighting a losing battle. Although drugs deaden the pain, I have a constant ache that affects my mobility and often distracts me. Kim would have me hold out for a cure, but this is her way of keeping the candle of life flickering when there is little hope.

The question, "What next?" comes naturally to mind. Is death the end of living, or is it the entry into another world?

In the fourth gospel, in the chapter that precedes the Last Supper, Jesus says to the apostles, Philip and Andrew, *"In truth, in very truth I tell you, a grain of wheat remains a solitary grain unless it falls to the ground and dies; but if it dies, it bears a rich harvest."*

Jesus holds out the promise of everlasting life, an assurance that reaches its peak in Revelation. John's language is highly pictorial, punctuated by voices and bursts of heavenly hymnody, especially when he himself experiences a mystical death and resurrection: *"Fear not, I am the first and the last, and the living one, I died, and behold I am alive for evermore."* Ecstatic words! But the best is yet to come. Life in the new Jerusalem is permanently incandescent: *"And the city had no need of the sun, neither of the moon, to shine in it: for the glory of God did lighten it,"* and suffering is a thing of the past. *"God shall wipe away all tears from their eyes; and there shall be no more death, neither sorrow, nor crying, neither shall there be any more pain: for the former things have passed away."*

John speaks of truths beyond human comprehension, of values beyond human estimation, of an alliance of love that, so to speak, brings man close to God. The imagery is powerful and uplifting, but if taken in some manner as literally true it is absurd. Yet instinct tells me, for the sake of one's wholeness, I must believe it.

44

PARIS

October 23

There is a silent partnership in the way that Kim and I do things together. Christians, it is true, know that they are *"strangers and pilgrims,"* have *"no continuing city,"* and that their *"citizenship"* is in heaven. But no matter how glorious our apokatastasis, the living is now. Fleeting and temporary it may be, but permanence was never part of God's plan. Although life stands under the shadow of death, it is not death that troubles me, but that time is slipping away, and we cannot hold on to a single moment.

Christianity has played no part in Kim's life. For Buddhists the "Son of Man" is just that—a son of man who, like the Buddha, has found enlightenment. Paul's demand for submission to a crucified person who was raised from the dead is incomprehensible to her (as it was a *"stumbling block"* for the Jews and *"foolishness unto the Greeks"*).

In contrast to Jesus, the Buddha needs no explanatory myths to reveal a position from which his life and death can be understood. After six years of fruitless wandering, he sat under a Bo-tree, passed into a state of superconsciousness and saw the "truth." For the next forty-five years he taught his program of deliverance from the miseries of existence. When he died, he did not ascend into godhood, but nirvana, an impersonal "nothingness" in which no new becoming can arise.

Although neither Jesus nor Buddha claimed to be anything but human, both have been given supernatural status. All religions have attempted to link their heroes to celestial events. Cosmic reveries have become incarnate in the figures of legend. Muhammad was transfigured by an apotheosis, and Gautama hypostatized into a universal presence. Christ was canonized by his posthumous followers as the final revelation. Humanity, in dreaming large, turns its idols into the likeness of gods.

PARIS

October 24

I am worried about Kim.

The Buddhist Tantra on death is so explicit that she knows exactly what is in store for her. She feels she has attracted so much bad karma that she will be reincarnated on the lowest rung of animal life. Believing that she might be reborn as an animal or another human being makes her extremely anxious. Since what is reincarnated is another new being, unconscious of any responsibility for former acts, any punishment for what was done in a former life is quite unjust. Reincarnation is a distressingly fanciful concept.

I can quite imagine beginning a new life, washed clean of all my defects, errors and failures, but it must be at the expense of the old life. The new self would be a self that is not me: what has happened to me would mean nothing to it: what happens to it can mean nothing to me. For Kim, a belief in "life after death" is not a consoling thought. On the contrary, reincarnation is an extremely painful way of returning to the eternal. Neither reincarnation nor Nirvana offer the vision of an eternal positive destiny for every man: nor is such a vision possible given the negative attitude that Buddhism takes toward the individual self.

Kim fears that her time as a prostitute has cancelled any merit she might have attracted. Her bad rebirth as an illegitimate child has convinced her that she has not overcome her previous karma. There is no easy palliative. Timothy's counsel, *"Have nothing to do with godless and silly myths,"* is all very well, but illogical fears are difficult to placate. What others think about them decides nothing whatever for the person who holds them. The feelings of guilt that stand behind so many of the demands we make of ourselves cause more distress that we think.

PARIS

October 25

This morning Kim and I walked to the Rue de Hanover to have lunch. Our pace is slower than other people's, but we are in no hurry. Sometimes our hands touch, but even if they do not, we keep close together. I am reminded of Christ's wonderful words, *"Why weepest thou?"* It assumes that happiness should come naturally to man. I have found it in the simplest of things: the glint of light on the Seine, the chestnut trees in the Tuilleries, the evening sunsets. The more time I spend with Kim, the more there has grown up in me a feeling of kinship with all that I see.

PARIS

October 27

Today Kim and I walked along the Seine as far as the Pont Neuf. It is not a long walk by normal standards, but we take our time. The air was very clear, the light soft, the Seine a glittering silver, and the grass in the Tuileries as green as the grass in a churchyard. Everything struck me as beautiful.

I have been reading Kim the Book of Job. Although the scale is that of myth, the immediate conflict is that of a deeply troubled mind and heart. It is a very Buddhist text in that it ends in the renunciation of any solution to the problem of existence. Death poses the same question to Job as it does for the Buddhist: whether life is worth living at all, because ultimately we all have to die, without the prospect of a better future than can be had here on earth. In the end everything was restored to Job in double portion—the poet's way of saying that Job's despair brought him back to God. But this is not an option for the Buddhist.

The earliest Buddhist Scriptures date from about A.D. 200, nearly 600 years after the Buddha's death. Because different schools wrote down different things, it is almost impossible to decide which Scriptures carry his actual sayings. But they all agree that the problem of suffering was his main concern. It compelled him to ask, "What is the self that is caught up in all this suffering?" and came to the startling conclusion that there is no "self." Man is nothing but a bundle of thoughts, emotions, and perceptions in such rapid flux that we have the impression of continuity, and thus of a "self" or an "I." There is suffering, but no one who suffers! The self we imagine surviving death is a phantom, even in life. At death this stream of mental energy is re-established in a new body, appropriate to its karma, and continues its shadowy identity as a separate "self." Death is transcended as illusory. But the price of this is that life is illusory as well.

Although Buddhism gives sensitive attention to the nature of suffering, its solution—to get rid of one's "I" or ego, is fated from the start. If there is no self, what is there to be saved? Nirvana is the end of suffering, but this promises no more than death itself offers.

If we compare Buddha's revelation with the statement,

"And the Lord God formed man and breathed into his nostrils the breath of life; and man became a living soul," agreement about man's nature and destiny scarcely seems possible.

The same goes for the Buddhist *"Absolute"* and God. The Old and New Testament call God *"a living God."* His "liveliness," which reveals itself first of all in creation, is in stark contrast to the fixed nature of the "Absolute," which remains motionless, aloof in its deadening silence. Faith, that encounter with a "Thou," is nonexistent.

PARIS

October 28

Kim does not talk about her past, but it stands between her and her peace of mind. The past is not something one can fight against. It will always get the better of us because it is part of our own hidden present. The karma that Kim feels she has brought on herself continues to trouble her. Karma does not forget, nor does it forgive.

PARIS

November 1

Another visit to the doctor this morning. He was very straightforward. He said there was no form of chemo or immunotherapy that can check a cancer that is so far advanced.

To distance one's self from life is not difficult. Old age and illness recommend it as a preparation for death. But I do not like to think about dying. As St. Augustine said, "Whatever comes to an end is too short."

I sometimes think that the supreme Christian virtue is simply getting through each day with one's belief in God intact.

PARIS

November 2

By late afternoon it is dark. The sky is already filling with winter.

I still take the keenest pleasure in walking with Kim, in spite of the effort it costs me. Our usual promenade is to the Quai des Tuileries and back. We walk hand in hand, often not speaking; and when we do, it is surprising how often we have been thinking the same thing.

In spite of my efforts I have not been able to dismantle the karmic pantheon of animals that haunt Kim's imagination. There can be no appeal to nirvana. *"Whatsoever ye shall ask the Father in my name, he will give it you,"* has no equivalent in Buddhist scripture. I have taken it upon myself to contact a Mahāyāna monk, Vajra-Siddhi, at the Centre Bouddhiste. I told him about the suffering Kim thinks she has brought upon herself, and the riot of phantasmal forms that populate her imagination. He said that such fears are not uncommon, and often lead to feelings of self-reproach. Although he maintained that release from the bondage of karma is possible only at death, he assured me that Buddhists could be reborn in one of the Buddhist heavens. This escape into other worlds, however imperfect from a Christian standpoint, is infinitely preferable to an endless cycle of rebirths.

Kim has agreed to see Vajra-Siddhi, although she is skeptical that karma can be undone in any form. On the other hand, we have Paul's words that man is naturally drawn towards God. If this is the case, then whatever our beliefs, our hearts will respond to the presence of that spirit which seeks our well-being.

PARIS

November 5

The Centre Bouddhiste de l'Ile de France is in the rue Condorcet. While Kim talked to Varja-Siddhi I waited in a nearby café. I ordered a coffee and listened to Edith Piaf. She sang about the "down and out" and those who live a double life, prostitutes and streetwalkers. There are many in Paris. It had been Kim's life too. A life with too little happiness.

Kim and Vajra-Siddhi were together for more than an hour. As soon as I saw her I could see from her step that she felt happier and that a weight had been lifted from her shoulders. She said that Vajra-Siddhi told her that we have a spiritual "orientation" that allows us to direct the "stream of life" and so avoid the worst effects of karma. He also said that every soul is identical with the all-pervading soul of the universe to which it belongs and to which it will return. The terms might be different, but the message is the same: *"whether we live therefore, or die, we are the Lord's."* I am hopeful that this will lead her to believe that only a providential God can be the God of all men and all religions.

All religions have fallen victim to the distortion of revelation. Buddha's insights have become entangled with karmic fatalism, and Vedic concepts of reincarnation. Christianity draws upon Judaic and Hellenic notions of life and life after death, complicating the simple commandment to love God and one's fellow man. We would do better, perhaps, to emulate the simplicity of those Buddhist monks, the symbol of whose faith is contained in one syllable: *Om*. Alongside their faith, the doctrines of religion are like fairy tales told to children.

PARIS

November 6

The change in Kim is remarkable. She walks with a lighter step. She is more confident and assured. I could not be happier.

In a simple way Vajra-Siddhi reassured her that her soul, previously held hostage to karma, will be restituted in blessedness. John's words, *"Most assuredly, I tell you, hereafter you will see heaven,"* do not sound so strange to her anymore.

PARIS

November 7

Today Kim and I went to Père-Lachaise.

This was a major excursion for me.

Père-Lachaise is no ordinary cemetery. It covers a huge area (44 hectares) and with more than 5000 trees is the largest park in Paris. Even so there are a staggering 300,000 bodies buried there and thousands more in the columbarium.

Our first stop was Chopin's tomb. His sepulchre is very modest, befitting someone with two graves (his heart lies in an urn in the Church of the Holy Cross in Krakow). Just before he died he thanked Abbé Jelowicki for leading him back to God. He then called out the names of Jesus and Mary, pressed his crucifix to his heart with the cry, "Now I am at the source of Blessedness," and gave up the ghost.

Given this exit, it is surprising that his memorial is

without resurrection imagery. In fact there is hardly a Christian symbol in Père-Lachaise. The memorial art consists almost entirely of sensual images of beautiful young women. Immortal and incorrupt, existing between the spiritual and the sensory, they bear witness to our longing for eternal life. While our lives run a single course, these surrogate mourners proclaim eternal renewal, reminding us that while birth prefigures death, death carries with it the hope of rebirth.

Kim did not know what to make of these female bodies. Their tacit appeal to the secrecy of eternity seemed far too improbable for her. Buddhist cemeteries are free of adornment and never display the female form. Since all but a few who die are destined to return to earth in one form or another, elaborate tombs are an extravagance. For my part I found these wingless seraphim a pleasure to look at. Besides being extremely engaging, they assure one, albeit provocatively, that at the conclusion of our exile in this world the bliss we once knew will be known again.

PARIS

November 15

I have not written anything the last few days.

When we returned from Père-Lachaise, I was exhausted. Not long after I felt a deep-seated pain, which quickened fears I had not long to live. Nothing can express the weariness that takes hold of me.

I told Kim that I must soon return to the Abbey. She insists that this is my home and that I stay here. But if I were to die in Paris, it would cause her no end of trouble.

In the meantime the days pass happily enough. When night falls I sometimes wonder how we have passed the hours, since we do very little. But pass they do, and all too quickly.

PARIS

November 18

I force myself to get up, walk about, and even venture outside (with Kim's support) for a short time each day. I was a good walker. But now, with great effort, I walk slowly, and less surely. With typical Buddhist pragmatism Kim tells me that as long as I can feel, I am alive, and to live for the present.

I try not to dwell on the future. I cannot ignore that I lose a little more of myself each day. When life touches death and we vanish from the surface of the earth, what then? Is death the end of living, or entry into another existence? *"If a man die, shall he live again?"* asked Job. But what does it mean "to die"? We speak of death as the end of life, but what is life? We really don't know what life is in its essence. We see only the outward signs of it. Death brings these signs to an end, but it may leave life's essence untouched.

In terms of our earthly existence, our lives are short-lived, and count for little when compared with the relatively permanent things around us. But if our lives are taken up into God's own existence, it is the world that passes away, and it is we who continue forever.

PARIS

November 20

Earlier this morning the wind was blowing a stiff gale. But now it has started to rain, not heavily, but a persistent drizzle. Kim goes about her business, silently and graceful, not because of me, but because this is her nature.

Loving Kim has brought to life the truth of Paul's statement that love is the essence of life— *"without love I am nothing."* This was not a leap of faith rooted in an unknowable impulse, but the consciousness of a divinely inspired love within himself. Loving someone is very different from loving God, but not completely. Both are a state of mind and heart. Both have their ups and downs, their withdrawals and returns, favours given and received. What we call love is deeper and more lasting than any existential realization of it.

Here on earth we know love through a glass darkly, but

behind the opaqueness we sense that it is more than just an emotion. John tells us that love is *"of the spirit"* and *"endureth into everlasting life"* eternity. It is part of our spiritual inheritance and cannot be lost. He goes on to say that the love we carry beyond death will not be a recreation of the love we experience in life, but *"perfected."* It is the nearest description we have of the life of the soul after death. /

It is significant that Jesus began many of his sayings about love with the word *Amen* ("Yes"). *"Amen, I say to you..."* And in John's gospel, when speaking about the indestructibility of love even more emphatically, with a twofold "Yes": *"Amen, amen, I say to you..."* In John the mutuality of love, *"I in you"* and *"you in me"* and finally *"I-in-you-in-me"* suffers no diminution. In this life, which is streaming towards death and eternity, there is an alliance of love that knows no end.

PARIS

November 21

The Abbot was right when he said that I was more likely to find Jesus in the street than the chapel, and the same could be said of God *("But the most high does not dwell in houses made with hands")*. If we are to know Jesus, we must see him as he saw himself, not as seen by the apostles, by Paul, by John, by the church.

The biblical Jesus wears many guises. He is the Messiah, anticipated by the Jews; he is the Son of Man, who is not expected, but lived amongst us; he is the risen Christ, appointed Lord of the universe, over both angels and nations, and he is the eternal Son, sent by God, through whom all things were made. When Jesus was asked which of these roles applied to him: *"Tell us, once and for all, whether or not you are the Christ,"* he replied, *"The Father and I are one"*...which does not answer the question. It was not answered for another four hundred years. In Chalcedon the bishops formulated a doctrine that is meaningless to most people: IN JESUS THERE IS ONE PERSON AND TWO NATURES. Jesus truly is God, but he is not just God, he is something else too; he is a man, as we are men. None of these expressions are used to describe Jesus in the New Testament. The word *person* does not occur, and there is no mention of two "natures" or "wills" in Jesus, divine or otherwise.

As long as the Christian message is a matter of statements, it can be accepted only if one is thinking, not on the level of experience or understanding, but on the level of belief.

PARIS

November 22

One day we will be ready to isolate the words of Jesus and reveal just how emancipatory they are. This may mean rejecting the dogmatism of Paul's epistles, credal formulas, and implausible doctrinal theories. Less buried, they will speak more clearly, calling us to recognize the truth about God and ourselves.

I never doubted that Jesus had a special relationship with God. He spoke of this when he said, *"I am never alone, the Father is always with me,"* and *"I have not spoken of myself; but the Father which sent me, he gave me a commandment, what I should say, and what I should speak."* No person and no prophet has ever made this claim. Such was his felt identity with God that of himself he could do "nothing," but does *"all that he sees the Father do."* Jesus is man, but God came visibly near to his person.

Jesus' mysterious unity of life with God gave him the most extraordinary insight into God's own nature, one never before experienced or known. In calling God *"Abba, Father,"* Jesus totally transformed our notion of eternal reality. The love that creates and promotes this seething universe of mass and energy, of chemical processes, of endlessly varied plant and animal life, of human intelligence and human love has a personal center! God is *"living and active"* and *"is for us."* The wholly other is at the same time the one who is wholly near!

PARIS

November 26

I have been in hospital.

Kim tells me that I collapsed and lost consciousness. I woke up to find myself in a hospital bed with Kim beside me. She had a real look of fear in her eyes. Death belongs to the dying, but it is those who love them that suffer the most.

The cancer has spawned metastic lesions through much of my body. To be more precise, it has invaded the tissues around the colon and metastasized to the liver. It was to be expected, but I did not think that it would spread so quickly or with such ill effect.

I can remember quite clearly, as I drifted in and out of consciousness, the heart-paralyzing sensation that I was going die. But the actual release, what I felt to be the final giving way, was a moment of well-being: a journey into timeless space that eclipsed all normal sensations. Everything I experienced occurred in an eternal "now"—an indescribable "oneness" of which I was a part. This was not felt as an out-of-body experience, but as a necessary displacement before the end.

To go beyond this is to experience the end of all experience. St. Teresa did. She saw herself being carried away as if by "a mighty eagle, knowing not wither, but with delight." Her vision went beyond anything that can be deduced from the natural consequence of dying. "God appears not to be content with thus attracting the soul to Himself in so real a way, but wishes to have the body also, though it be mortal. Oftimes the soul is absorbed—or, so to speak, more correctly, the Lord absorbs it in Himself; and when He has held it thus for a moment, the will alone remains in union with him. It is a soft flight, a delicious flight, a noiseless flight."

And in this delicious flight, she remains conscious that her self is preserved, her identity unbroken. "This vision though imaginary, I did never see with my bodily eyes, nor, indeed, any other, but only with the eyes of the soul." She ends by saying that in heaven the soul does not see only God, but everything in God, and becomes one with everything visible and invisible, and so acquires consciousness of its own divinity. Death is the soul's liberation, an orgasmic moment, an ejaculatory flash into eternal bliss.

Her mystical experience is close to Paul's own revelations. In Colossians and Ephesians the hymnic language is high-flown, suggesting exciting possibilities in the supernatural world. In Romans, death is the *"baptismal"* separation of spirit from matter. Resurrection is not a day of assembly but the bestowal of a new form to our spirit (*"soma pneumatic"*).

Paul denies the nakedness of a merely spiritual existence, and asserts the spiritually transformed total personality of man. In some sense we are both ourselves and distinct from ourselves, a *"new creation."* This corresponds to the apparition stories about Jesus. All agree that he was experienced in his total personality, including the bodily expression of his being: *"We have seen the Lord"* and *"we know him now."*

Mystical gifts, touching God and being touched by Him, the naked burning encounter—no doubt these happen. They happened to Paul and St. Teresa. The saints' missions, mysteriously, are answers of heaven to the questions of earth. Whatever we make of them they stretch the soul's imagination and reveal our hidden, unconscious yearnings.

PARIS

November 27

Paul and St. Teresa replace the threat of being thrown out of existence with the promise of a new beginning without losing our sense of identity. It is not the soul's immortality that we desire, with some sort of body or spirit-covering, but to go on living in a way that does not put an end to self-consciousness. Paul's statement that we are "*preserved entire*" answers that hope exactly.

In Buddhism the super-sensorial contact with the "Beyond" leads to dissolution of the person in to the vast anonymity of an "Absolute." Death is a flight into nothing, a silent void that is beyond all relative, individual being. Extinction puts an end to suffering, but it also puts an end to man. Because the Buddha neither affirmed nor denied the existence of a Supreme Personal Being but favored an impersonal salvation into the nothingness of Nirvana, the dead fall into silence: a silence which is not the indefinable moment of the begetting and birth of the new man, where a true spiritual seeing and hearing become possible, but the chill silence of nothingness.

Everything is decided by the question whether God *is*.

PARIS

November 29

J esus said:
> "He that heareth my word, and believeth on him that sent me, hath everlasting life, and shall not come into condemnation; but is passed from death unto life."

But did Jesus speak with God's voice? Luke thought so. *"Did we not feel our hearts on fire as he talked with us on the road...?"*

Unless there is something which at all costs *must* be, and that holds the power of eternity within itself, life is nothing but a meaningless episode on a twirling speck of cosmic rock. We, actors in the drama of human living, are but stagehands. The setting is magnificent, the lighting superb, the costumes wonderful, but there is no play.

I have to believe that God is in complicity with the

human spirit and that his covenant is binding. *"For whether we live, we live unto the Lord; and whether we die, we die unto the Lord: whether we live therefore, or die, we are the Lord's."* These words say all there is to be said; nothing can be added to them.

PARIS

December 1

I miss the sunlight, and while there is little azure in the sky, I hope that I might still feel its warmth. Kim tells me that the lime trees are almost bare of leaves, and the air carries the scent of autumn fires. I fear that my walking days are over. Kim is very patient with me. She does not let me forget that there is much that we still share together.

During the last few weeks I have felt more of an invalid than a man. But even when one has little or nothing left, when one's only achievement consists in just staying alive, it is still possible to find happiness. It takes very little: the nearness of someone you love, the memory of those rare and lovely moments that have graced your life.

PARIS

December 2

There are minutes, hours even, when everything in the world strikes me as being without purpose.

It was St. Ignatius Loyola who gave the advice: act as though results depended exclusively on you, but await the results as though they depended entirely on God. I try to ignore the closure that has set in and the feeling that life is contracting around me. But it does not lessen the fear that death will bring decrease and disappearance, the slippage of everything into nothingness.

"*Is God asleep?*" asks the psalmist. "*O Lord, how long shall I cry for help, and thou will not hear?*" The Buddha uttered a similar cry, "*Can there be blessing, if everything that is, suffers?*" Death is a dreadful ending. A human being is torn away from us: what remains is a body locked in the icy stillness of death. There no longer exists any hope of a relationship. All the bonds of human contact have come to an end. Nothing is more final than a human body bereft of life.

Suffering is the scarlet thread that runs though our history. It is destructively real, a hurt beyond tears. But there is more, namely God. *"I will not leave you desolate: I will come to you."* This does not make light of what is grievous in human experience, but it does rob failure and suffering of its presumption to have the last word.

PARIS

December 3

Yesterday I felt acutely depressed. For no apparent reason I was overcome, as if by a wave of nausea, that bodily death has no outcome. Even St. Augustine, who believed that "we do not die utterly," was overcome with despair at the death of his mother. Ironically it was not Augustine, but his mother, who came to terms with death in the belief that, "Nothing is far off from God, neither is there any cause too fear."

This is the faith one must try to emulate, the faith that gives the courage to face death knowing that neither death nor life, nor things present, nor things to come, can separate us from the love of God. Love is the quintessence of man's spirit, and perhaps of divinity itself. *"He who abides in love abides in God, and God with him."*

Love is not an event that can be isolated and described. It is always a movement in, with, and under other states of mind. It is our link with the eternal: the one thing which nothing can undo, and which nothing can detach itself from.

PARIS

December 4

I leave for England tomorrow.

I am in a sorry state: weak, no appetite, and any movement leaves me exhausted. The medications I am taking for pain and nausea are only partly effective. I know that I am rapidly going downhill. This is the moment I have been dreading, but it must be faced.

Kim and I have promised each other that there will be no tears: that what we have shared will always be with us. But in my heart I will miss her deeply. In this world love rarely has a happy ending. In one way or another, someone is always left behind.

Kim made me feel that my life was just beginning, not reaching its end. Had we not met, I would have died before I had begun to live. She took me into her life, and gave me her arms, knowing that the little I could give her was fleeting and conditional. Some things we can never repay, but simply count ourselves lucky.

I have given Kim the annuity that was left to me. It is little enough but will carry her through the worst of times. She has spoken about working for Emmaüs, a homeless charity. A good sign. If I have helped make life a little more beautiful, more complete, and more satisfactory for her, then my life has not been wasted.

St. Benedict Monastery

December 6

For the last forty-eight hours I have slept the sleep of Endymion. I remember arriving at the monastery and the Abbot helping me to my cell, but nothing more.

How quickly the past withdraws itself. Kim, Paris, our walks in the Tuileries, belong to another age. I can scarcely recall our time together, but I feel her presence.

My cell is familiar. There is no strangeness in my return. It is late morning, but my room is deep in shadow. The Benedictine instinct for devotion presumes that a light subdued to gloom alone befits the attitude of prayer. But I do not pray. I am content to listen. The monk's voices ebb and flow like music.

St. Benedict Monastery

December 7

The brothers are at vespers.

In St. Benedict the Office includes a vigil of Old Testament canticles.

"You sing; who listens to you? You serve; who sees?"

Does anyone feel that we have lit a fire? That light and warmth spread out from our cloister?

Experiences may be transmitted by language, others by silence; and then there are those that cannot be transmitted, not even by silence, and it is their fruit that we offer to the world.

ST. BENEDICT
MONASTERY

December 9

The Abbot is never far from my bedside.

Because he is convinced that death is the beginning of life with God, he speaks without tears or pity. He has seen death may times before. His words are tempered by the assurance that nothing can separate us from the love of God. "Whatever is to come, we have that certainty of knowing and of being known, no matter how dark the night." His conviction comes not from words revealed by Jesus, but in response to the presence in Jesus of the same God whose presence he feels within himself.

St. Benedict Monastery

December 10

I f death brings nothing new and only puts an end to life, and if God corresponds to absolutely nothing real, I know that in so far as I have lived in a way which seems to me to be asked for by Him, I have lived life more fully than I might otherwise have known.

St. Benedict Monastery

December 12

Isaiah said, *"Thy dead shall live; thy bodies rise."* Absolutely unmagical, unmythical, unspeculative, even unmystical, these words are a confirmation that death is the gateway to a new beginning, of an alliance and love, so to speak, that will bring us to God.

St. Benedict Monastery

December 18

This morning the Abbot asked me to pray with him.

We said the little-known prayer for healing which ends with the words "... and help me always to believe that what happens to me here is of little account if you hold me in eternal life, my Lord and my God."

Then he said, "Perhaps the deepest reason why we are afraid of death is because we do not know who we are."

ST. BENEDICT MONASTERY

December 25

Today is Christmas, but the belfry is silent. The monastery chapel has no bells. St. Benedict had no use for festivity and little for merriment. But even when solitude is piled upon solitude and silence added to silence, eyes will stray from the Cross and memory return to the past.

Kim is more emotion than appearance. The memories that linger, like colors at sunset, have begun to fade. But nothing can eclipse what we shared. Of all the motions and affection of the soul, only love is unaffected by death. This may sound romantic and mystical, but it is no more than a restatement of Matthew's words that God will restore all things.

St. Benedict
Monastery

December 26

"**P**eace I leave with you; my peace I give you. Do not let your hearts be troubled and do not be afraid."
Sublime words.

St. Benedict Monastery

December 28

The reality of not physically existing is very real to me now. All that I am is becoming concentrated in the immanent simplicity of my mind. A glide into invisible reaches is the next step. To look beyond this is to call forth images that have the quality of inaccessible distances.

St. Benedict Monastery

December 29

I woke to find Brother Simon washing my body. I feel a great languor, as if a heavy blanket has been placed over me. He did not have to tell me that I was on edge of death. I know in my heart that I have reached the outermost limit. Everything I am, everything I had been, and everything I aimed at or wished for, has been stripped from me. All that remains is the experience of myself as myself, but moving ever further away from life, towards an ever-present beyond that carries existence within it.

St. Benedict Monastery

December 30

I have made my confession.

"*Confiteor Deo omnipotenti, beatae Mariae semper Virgini, beato Michaeli Archangelo, beato Ioanni Baptistae, sanctis Apostolis Petro et Paulo, et omnibus Sanctis, quia peccavi nimis cogitatione, verbo et opere: mea culpa, mea culpa, mea maxima culpa...*"

Unto God belong the issues of death. I pray that he not hide his face from me or put me away in anger.

Know that I love you and that when death comes I will have found my way to something new.

St. Benedict
Monastery

December 31

The waiting is almost over.

Before this day is ended, I will know the truth about everything.

Next time we speak we will have no need of words. All our missing years will be pieced together and we will live in glory.

"Fear not, for I have redeemed thee, I have called thee by thy name; thou art mine."

Author's Note

While carrying out research for my book *A Carnival of Lies,* Auschwitz-Birkenau was one of several death camps I visited. While walking through the remains of Krema 2 in Birkenau, I had a mental picture of hundreds of men, women, and children walking down the concrete steps and into the gas chamber. For a moment I felt myself among them, experiencing their confusion and fear. Until then I had given little thought to the meaning of death: but the experience of being drawn into their lives compelled me to consider whether death is the end of our personal existence, or, as St. Paul would have us believe, the beginning of life in God. *An Unholy Love* is the result.

NOTES

References are listed in the order of their appearance in the journal entries.

London, September 20
"God will have mercy on whom He will have mercy; so then it is not of him that willeth, not of him that runneth, but of God that showeth mercy."—Romans 9:15-16

"For I would have you know, brethren, that the gospel preached by me is not according to man, for I did not receive it from man but through a revelation of Jesus Christ."—1 Corinthians 15:1

London, September 21
"eat the labour of thine hands"—Psalms 128:2

"Thus says the Lord: By waiting and calm, you shall be saved. In quiet and trust lies your strength."—Isaiah 30:15

Paris, September 26
"Who is this that darkens counsel by words without insight?"—Job 38:2

"by whom are all things, and we by him"—1 Corinthians 8:6

Paris, September 27
"I was laid hold of by Jesus Christ."—Philippians 3:12

"raised from the dead and dieth no more"—Romans 6:9

"For there is no other save me; I am Alpha and Omega, the beginning and the end, the first and the last."—Revelation 1:8

<u>Paris, September 28</u>
"And saying, 'The time is fulfilled, and the kingdom of God is at hand'"—Mark 1:15

"King of the Jews"; *"You have said it"*—Mark 15:2

"set at the right hand of God"—Acts 2:34

"to the kingdom of his beloved Son"—Colossians 1:13

"I alone am God, the Creator of all, and apart from me there is no other."—Isaiah 45:5

<u>Paris, September 29</u>
"other gods"—Deuteronomy 5:7

"He that believeth on me, believeth not on me, but on him that sent me."—John 12:44

"He has entered heaven itself, now to appear in the presence of God on our behalf."—Hebrews 9:24

<u>Paris, September 30</u>
"But to us there is but one God, the Father, of whom are all things, and we in him; and one Lord Jesus Christ, by whom are all things, and we by him"—1 Corinthians 8:6

<u>Paris, October 20</u>
"In truth, in very truth I tell you, a grain of wheat remains a solitary grain unless it falls to the ground and dies; but if it dies, it bears a rich harvest."—John 12:24

"Fear not, I am the first and the last, and the living one, I died, and behold I am alive for evermore."—Revelation 1:17

"And the city had no need of the sun, neither of the moon, to shine in it: for the glory of God did lighten it"—Revelation 22:5

"God shall wipe away all tears from their eyes; and there shall be no more death, neither sorrow, nor crying, neither shall there be any more pain: for the former things have passed away."—Revelation 21:4

Paris, October 23
"strangers and pilgrims"—Hebrews 11:13

"no continuing city"—Hebrews 13:14

"citizenship"—Hebrews 11:16

"stumbling block"—1 Corinthians 1:23

"foolishness unto the Greeks"—1 Corinthians 1:23

Paris, October 24
"Have nothing to do with godless and silly myths"—1 Timothy 1:4

Paris, October 25
"Why weepest thou?"—John 20:13

Paris, October 27
"And the Lord God formed man and breathed into his nostrils the breath of life; and man became a living soul"—Genesis 2:7

"a living God"—Deuteronomy 5:26

Paris, November 2
"Whatsoever ye shall ask the Father in my name, he will give it you"—John 16:23

Paris, November 5
"whether we live therefore, or die, we are the Lord's"—Romans 14:8

Paris, November 5
"Most assuredly, I tell you, hereafter you will see heaven"—John 1:51

Paris, November 18
"If a man die, shall he live again?"—Job 14:14

Paris, November 20
"without love I am nothing"—1 Corinthians 13:1-2

"of the spirit"—1 John 3:24

"endureth into everlasting life"—John 6:27

"perfected"—Hebrews 10:14

Paris, November 21
"But the most high does not dwell in houses made with hands"—Acts 7:48

"Tell us, once and for all, whether or not you are the Christ," he replied, *"The Father and I are one."*—John 10:24, 30

Paris, November 22
"I am never alone, the Father is always with me"—John 8:29

"I have not spoken of myself; but the Father which sent me, he gave me a commandment, what I should say, and what I should speak."; *"all that he sees the Father do"*—John 8:28

"living and active"—1 Timothy 6:17

"is for us"—1 Timothy 4:10

<u>Paris, November 26</u>
"We have seen the Lord"—John 20:25

"we know him now"—John 14:7

<u>Paris, November 27</u>
"preserved entire"—1 Corinthians 15:42

<u>Paris, November 29</u>
"He that heareth my word, and believeth on him that sent me, hath everlasting life, and shall not come into condemnation; but is passed from death unto life."—John 5:24

"Did we not feel our hearts on fire as he talked with us on the road...?"—Luke 24:32

"For whether we live, we live unto the Lord; and whether we die, we die unto the Lord: whether we live therefore, or die, we are the Lord's."—Romans 14:8

<u>Paris, December 2</u>
"Is God asleep?" asks the psalmist. *"O Lord, how long shall I cry for help, and thou will not hear?"*—Habakkuk 1:2

"I will not leave you desolate: I will come to you."—John 14:18

<u>Paris, December 3</u>
"He who abides in love abides in God, and God with him."—1 John 4:16

<u>St. Benedict Monastery, December 12</u>
"Thy dead shall live; thy bodies rise."—Isaiah 26:19

St. Benedict Monastery, December 26

"Peace I leave with you; my peace I give you. Do not let your hearts be troubled and do not be afraid."—John 14:27

St. Benedict Monastery, December 31

"Fear not, for I have redeemed thee, I have called thee by thy name; thou art mine."—Isaiah 43:1

A
CARNIVAL
OF
LIES

VERNON L. ANLEY

The Gestapo arrested my father in Berlin
in the summer of 1933.
When he asked why, he was told,
"We do not give reasons."

This fictional autobiography of an undercover agent in
Nationalist Socialist Germany portrays with unembellished
clarity the horrors of the Nazi regime, contrasted to those
whose faith in humankind—even when they perish—
outlasts those terrible years. **Highly recommended.**
ALAN SCOTT, CVO, CBE, lately Governor of the Cayman Islands

Totalitarianism has never seemed more subtle, insidious, and
in the end more terrifying. **An outstanding book, beautifully
written and absorbing.**
J.K. TAPLIN

Anley's nightmarish narrative about a nation led into infamy
gallops on at a pace and style guaranteed to hold the reader's
attention from the start. **A powerful story of human survival
against all odds and a triumph of hope over despair.**
RAYMOND ZALA

ABOUT THE AUTHOR

DR. VERNON L. ANLEY was educated in Australia and in England. After leaving university he worked for the Ministry of Overseas Development in the West Indies before resuming an academic career in Europe and the Far East.

He has coauthored a number of academic books, written travel guides on the Hejaz and Yemen, radio scripts, and articles on linguistics and education.

A Carnival of Lies, a novel about the complex developments in Germany between 1939 and 1945, is an outstanding work from which no one interested in the subject can fail to profit. His visits to Hitler's death camps in Germany, Poland, and Austria raised question about human nature and death which he attempts to answer in An *Unholy Love*.

www.ingramcontent.com/pod-product-compliance
Lightning Source LLC
Chambersburg PA
CBHW060844250626
47162CB00005B/2152